KU-256-115

Mr Croc Rocks

Written and illustrated
by **Frank Rodgers**

A & C Black • London

LV 32905882

LIVERPOOL LIBRARIES

First published in paperback 2009
First published 2008 by
A & C Black Publishers Ltd
38 Soho Square, London, W1D 3HB

www.acblack.com

Text and illustrations copyright © 2008 Frank Rodgers

The right of Frank Rodgers to be identified as the
author and illustrator of this work has been asserted by him
in accordance with the Copyrights, Designs and Patents Act 1988.

ISBN 978-0-7136-8422-3

A CIP catalogue for this book is available from the British Library.

All rights reserved. No part of this publication may be reproduced in
any form or by any means – graphic, electronic or mechanical, including
photocopying, recording, taping or information storage and retrieval
systems – without the prior permission in writing of the publishers.

This book is produced using paper that is made from wood grown in
managed, sustainable forests. It is natural, renewable and recyclable.
The logging and manufacturing processes conform to the
environmental regulations of the country of origin.

Printed and bound in Singapore by Tien Wah Press (Pte) Ltd

Chapter One

Mr Croc was happy.
He hummed to himself as he made a
huge pile of sardine sandwiches.

He was going to watch his favourite TV
show – CROC STAR.

Mr Croc switched
on the TV.

Mr Croc had a terrible memory.
He had only remembered to watch the
show because he had put notes to himself
everywhere.
The notes all said the same thing…

The show began and on came the star –
Rocky Alligator.

His smile
is almost
as nice
as mine!

Watch
CROC
STAR
today!

Mr Croc had one hundred, shiny teeth.
He thought he had the best smile in
the whole world.

Rocky Alligator was brilliant.
He danced…

he sang…

and he played guitar.

Mr Croc was very impressed.

"I'm going to be like Rocky Alligator," said Mr Croc when the show was over.

I'm going to be on TV.

He put a CD into the CD player.

I'll start by dancing.

"But wait a minute," he said. "I'm sure there's something I've forgotten."

Mr Croc thought hard.

Chapter Two

The music started and Mr Croc began to jump up and down.

Mr Croc ended up on the floor all tied in knots.

"I've just remembered what it was I forgot," he said.

He got to his feet.

"But I know what I *can* do," he said.

He put on a Rocky Alligator CD and
began to sing along with Rocky…
at the top of his voice.

Mr Croc's singing wasn't just bad…
it was *awful*! It was so awful that
Mr Gloss dropped his paint pot…

Mr Green chopped
the heads off
his roses…

and Miss Siam
spilled ink on
her drawing.

But Mr Croc was pleased with himself.

That sounded excellent !

He smiled his lovely smile in the mirror.

I'll soon be a star on TV. I must tell Mr Hound.

Chapter Three

That afternoon, Mr Croc put on his jacket
and went into town.

His best friend, Mr Hound, was looking
in a shop window.

"I'm going to be a star on TV," said
Mr Croc with excitement.
"Are you?" said Mr Hound, surprised.

"As soon as they hear me singing," said
Mr Croc.

He began to sing at the top of his voice.

It was so awful that
Mr Hound covered
his ears…

and Mrs Poodle
dropped a glass
vase she had just
bought.

Luckily, Mr Hound
sprang to the rescue.

"Your singing gave me a fright, Mr Croc!" said Mrs Poodle.

"I'm sorry," said Mr Croc.

"Oh dear," said Mr Croc.

"No," said Mr Hound.

But at least you'll look like one at the fancy dress party next week.

"I'd forgotten all about that!" said Mr Croc.

I'm going as Rocky Alligator. I've already made the costume.

So, you're right, Mr Hound. At least I will look like a star.

Just then, Mr Croc caught sight of a
guitar in the shop window.
He smiled his lovely smile.
"Ah ha!" he said. "Perhaps I could be
on TV after all."

I could play the guitar!

"Oh dear," muttered Mr Hound.

Chapter Four

Mr Croc bought the guitar and rushed home.

He began to practise straight away.

At first, he wasn't very good.

Everyone covered their ears.

But, as the days went by, he soon got better. Toes began to tap and smiles began to spread.

Mr Croc plays very well.

He's hot stuff.

Yes, he's cool!

In Mr Croc's house, the telephone rang.

It was Mr Hound.

"The fancy dress party has started,"
said Mr Hound.

Mr Croc quickly put on his Rocky
Alligator costume and dashed out.

Although Mr Croc was a bit late for the party, he had a great time.

He won a prize for his costume.
"You look exactly like Rocky Alligator!"
said Miss Siam.

You could be his twin!

Mr Croc was very pleased.

Walking home after the party, he began to daydream that he really *was* Rocky Alligator.

So he wasn't surprised when someone called out his name…

As Mr Croc turned round, a TV producer
rushed up.

"There you are!" said the TV producer.
"We thought you weren't coming!"

Chapter Five

Before Mr Croc knew what was
happening, he was hurried into a TV
studio…

and pushed on to the stage.

The audience clapped loudly.
"Rocky!" they cried.

Suddenly, Mr Croc realised the mistake.
"But I'm not Rocky!" he said to the
TV producer.

The TV producer laughed, thinking it was a joke. "Of course you are," he said.

You're our very own Mr Croc Star!

The band laughed, too, and Mr Croc was handed a guitar.

"Let's go, Rocky," said the drummer.
"We'll do 'Rock and Roll'."

Mr Croc had been
practising the song all day.
Without thinking, he began to play.

He sounded just like
Rocky Alligator.
He was terrific.
He was groovy.
He was cool.

The audience went wild.

"This is great!" thought Mr Croc.
"Everyone loves my guitar playing…"

He stepped up to the mike and began to sing at the top of his voice.

It wasn't just bad… it was *awful.*

The band stopped playing.

The audience fell silent.

Mr Croc stopped singing.
"You're not Rocky Alligator!" said the
TV producer, hurrying on to the stage.

Chapter Six

Just then, Rocky Alligator arrived.
"Sorry I'm late, everyone," he said.
He held up a bandaged thumb.

The TV producer told Rocky Alligator
what had happened.
Rocky laughed and shook Mr Croc's
hand.

"Not at all," said Mr Croc.

"Oh no, you won't!" cried Rocky.
He held up his thumb. "As you can see,
I can't play my guitar…"

…so will you stay and play it for me, please?

We'll be the CROC STAR twins!

Mr Croc didn't need asking twice.
He played guitar while Rocky danced
and sang.

The audience loved it. Everyone said it
was the best CROC STAR show they had
ever seen.

"Rocky! Rocky! Rocky!" they chanted.

Mr Croc! Mr Croc! Mr Croc!

After the show, Rocky Alligator asked
Mr Croc to join his band.

"We'll tour the world in trains, boats
and planes," he said.

"Oh dear," said Mr Croc. "It sounds like such a lot of work."

He shook his head.

"Thank you, Mr Alligator," said Mr Croc. "But I don't want to be a star after all."

"All right," said Rocky Alligator. "But I'd like to thank you in some way."

Mr Croc smiled his lovely smile.

So the next week, Mr Croc and his friends had front-row seats for the show.

Mr Hound, Miss Siam, Mrs Poodle, Mr Green and Mr Gloss had a wonderful evening.

When Rocky Alligator invited Mr Croc on stage to play guitar for one last time, they all cheered.

Once again, Mr Croc was brilliant.
Toes were tapping everywhere.

At the end of the song, as the last note
faded from Mr Croc's guitar, the whole
audience leapt to its feet.

"Mr Croc rocks!" they shouted.

"Thank you," said Mr Croc. "It was nice being a star for a little while…"

Mr Croc smiled his lovely smile, showing all of his one hundred, shiny teeth.